# This Topsy and Tim book belongs to

_____

Published by Ladybird Books Ltd
80 Strand London WC2R ORL
A Penguin Company

5 7 9 10 8 6

© Jean and Gareth Adamson MCMXCVII
This edition MMIV

ISBN-13: 978-1-84422-314-5

Printed in China

# Topsy + Tim

# Little Lost Rabbit

**Jean** and **Gareth Adamson**

When Topsy and Tim looked out of the window on Wednesday morning, they saw a black and white rabbit nibbling their marigolds.

Topsy and Tim heard the doorbell ring.
They ran downstairs and opened the
front door.
Mr Fen who lived next door was there,
holding the rabbit.
"Look what I've found," he said.

The rabbit looked at Topsy and Tim
and wiggled his nose.
"Please, may I hold it?" asked Topsy.
The rabbit sat quietly with its front
paws on Topsy's arm.
"It's very tame," said Mummy.
"I wonder who it belongs to?"
"We'll have to ask the neighbours,"
said Mr Fen.

Dad found a big box for the rabbit
to sit in.
"Would it like some of my cornflakes?"
asked Tim.

When it was time to go to playgroup,
Topsy and Tim wanted to stay and
play with the rabbit.

"Come on, now," said Mummy. "You can tell Miss Maypole all about the rabbit. One of the children at playgroup might know who it belongs to."

"Does anyone know who might have lost a black and white rabbit?"
Miss Maypole asked the children.
"Topsy and Tim found one in their garden this morning."
"It could be Mr Fishwick," said Lynne.
"He lives next door to us. He keeps black and white rabbits."

When Mummy came to take Topsy and Tim home, Miss Maypole told her about Mr Fishwick.
"We'll see if the rabbit belongs to him this afternoon," said Mummy.
Topsy looked as if she would cry.
Tim dragged his toes along the pavement all the way home.

When they got home, the rabbit met them at the door. It had climbed out of its box.

All through lunch, the rabbit played round the table legs. It sat up on its back paws so Topsy and Tim could tickle its ears.

After lunch, Mummy put the rabbit
inside her zip-bag with a lettuce leaf
to nibble. She closed the zip, all but
a few centimetres.
The rabbit poked its wiggling nose
out of the gap.
"I don't want the rabbit to go,"
said Topsy.
"I don't, either," said Tim.
They were both trying hard not to cry.
"If the rabbit does belong to
Mr Fishwick, perhaps he'll let
you visit it," said Mummy.

Mr Fishwick didn't live far away.
Mummy took the rabbit out of
the zip-bag. "Yes," he said, "that's
my rabbit. He got out this morning
when I opened the hutch."
Topsy and Tim began to cry.

Mr Fishwick looked thoughtful.
"I think my rabbit hutch is getting
too crowded," he said. "Do you know
anyone who could give this rabbit a
good home?"
"We can! We can!" said Topsy
and Tim together.

When they got home again, Mummy said, "Now that he is your rabbit, you must both look after him. You must see that he has water to drink and the right things to eat."

"I'll get him some food now," said Tim.

"And I'll get him some water," said Topsy.

"Is that rabbit still here?" said Dad,
when he came home from work.
Topsy and Tim told him the good news.
"We must give him a name," said Dad.
"We've given him one," said Topsy.
"It's Wiggles," said Tim, "because his
nose wiggles."

"Well then," said Dad, "we must give Wiggles a house."
He took Topsy and Tim to the shed, and they found some wood and wire netting to make a rabbit hutch.

Wiggles sat in his new hutch and wiggled his nose.

# Point to the rabbit pairs.

Help Wiggles to find the way to his new home.

Tell the story.

Which animals are big?
Which are little?

Match each animal below to something
that rhymes with its name.